D0351060

Louise Leblanc

# Maddie Needs Her Own Life

Illustrated by Marie-Louise Gay
Translated by Sarah Cummins

**First Novels**

Formac Publishing Company Limited
Halifax, Nova Scotia

Formac Publishing Company Limited acknowledges the support
of the Cultural Affairs Section, Nova Scotia Department of
Tourism and Culture. We acknowledge the financial support of
the Government of Canada through the Book Publishing Industry
Development Program (BPIDP) for our publishing activities.

We acknowledge the support of the Canada Council for the Arts
for our publishing program.

---

**National Library of Canada Cataloguing in Publication Data**
  Leblanc, Louise, 1942-
  [Sophie veut vivre sa vie. English]
  Maddie needs her own life
      (First novels ; #40)
      Translation of: Sophie veut vivre sa vie.
      ISBN 0-88780-551-5 (bound)
      ISBN 0-88780-550-7 (pbk.)

I. Gay, Marie-Louise  II. Cummins, Sarah  III. Title.  IV. Series
PS8573.E25S665713 2001    jC843'.54    C2001-902566-1
PZ7.L4694Ma 2001

---

Formac Publishing
Company Limited
5502 Atlantic Street
Halifax, Nova Scotia B3H 1G4
www.formac.ca

Printed and bound in Canada

Distributed in the United States by:
Orca Book Publishers
P.O. Box 468 Custer, WA
USA 98240-0468

Distributed in the UK by
Roundabout Books (a division
of Roundhouse Publishing Ltd.)
31 Oakdale Glen, Harrogate,
N Yorks. HG1 2JY

Table of Contents

*To Hélène Leblanc,*
*for her collaboration*

# 1
# Same Old, Same Old

Sunday morning. I was so bored I could feel my hair turning grey. It looked like the afternoon was going to be just as dismal.

I phoned all my friends. No relief.

Patrick was stuck at home, forced to study. Nicholas was helping his parents in the corner store.

"I have to stock up on candy," he told me. "That's how I keep you guys swarming around me like flies."

Poor Nicholas. He doesn't have much self-confidence. I wondered if he would still be our friend if he didn't offer us treats. So I phoned Clementine to see what she thought.

"Maddie, please get off the phone," my father called. "Your mother may be trying to reach us."

"She only went out for an hour!"

"Stop arguing and come here and help me."

Whenever my dad is fixing lunch, the whole world has to stop and help him.

"When are we going to eat?" whined Alexander, walking into the kitchen.

"WAHHH!" shrieked my

little sister Angelbaby.

That meant, "I want to be fed right now!" I told my dad I would take care of it. He accepted and assigned Alexander the task he had earmarked for me: chopping an onion.

"You guys are cooking without me!" Julian showed up. "That's not nice! I know how to cook too!"

To prove his point, he told Alexander, "Forget about your knife! You need that handy dandy machine that chops an onion faster than you can say 'Draw!'"

He illustrated by pulling an imaginary pistol from an imaginary holster.

I left them to it. I accom-

plished my task by giving
Angelbaby a couple of
cookies, and then I phoned
Clementine.

Last chance to save my day.

By five o'clock in the afternoon, I finally got out. I felt stifled! I did not save my day. Clementine had a karate class. At home it was the same boring routine.

Angelbaby swallowed a cookie whole. She choked and then she threw up.

Using the handy dandy onion-chopper, my brothers went through a whole bag of onions. My mother did not appreciate this wastefulness.

When I complained that I had nothing to do, she sent me to my room to tidy up.

"There's plenty to do! The only thing in your room that's tidy is your school bag!"

It was so depressing. So I went out.

"Hi, Maddie! Did you manage to escape from the loony bin?" I heard a mocking voice behind me.

It was Nicholas. The last thing I needed was his snide remarks!

"I came out for a little peace and quiet, Nicholas, so butt out, would you?"

"Hey, Nick, she's really telling you off!"

There was a guy with Nicholas. He was something else. He must have been at least 13 years old, and his eyes were magnetic, and—

Beep-beep! Beep-beep!

He had a cell phone! Wow!

He answered the phone and moved away. Nicholas raised his thumb in approval.

I wondered how a guy like that could be friends with Nicholas.

He must really like candy!

# 2
## Stepping Out

His name was Jesse. That was all I could find out about Nicholas's friend. I was dying to learn more, so math class seemed even more boring than usual.

When Mrs. Spiegel turned around to write a problem on the board, Nicholas signalled to me. "Important message for Maddie!" he said, throwing a little rolled-up ball of paper.

It landed on Clementine's desk, and she kept it! Honestly, she should mind her own business!

"It's for me," I hissed. "Didn't you hear?"

"Very well," Mrs. Spiegel swivelled around. "Since this is such an important missive, I will ask Clementine to read it aloud."

That was appalling—an invasion of my privacy! The note was nobody's business but mine!

"*I have to talk to you*," Clementine revealed to the entire class.

Whew! Not much in that to interest Spiegel the Eagle.

"That is indeed an important message," she said. "But it was sent to the wrong person. Clementine, please deliver it to Nicholas, from me."

* * *

At recess, I chewed Clementine out.

"You'll do anything to suck up!"

"What else could I do?" Little Miss Perfect tried to defend herself.

"You're being unfair to Clementine," Patrick chimed

in. "She kept the note to save your skin."

"It wasn't her decision to make!"

"That's right!" Nicholas said. "Adults have too much power. You have to stand up for yourself. Come over here, Maddie. I don't want the whole class to hear what I have to tell you."

This wasn't the old Nicholas I had known. He had changed.

"That's because of Jesse," he told me.

"Is he really your friend?!"

"The best! He showed me that I'm really somebody, only I didn't realize it."

"How did he know?"

"He watched me. He comes to the store a lot. He saw that

my parents were, like, smothering my personality. He's really observant. Now, about you, for example—"

"He talked about me!!!"

"He thinks you're great. He says you're a girl with character. He thinks you must like action."

"Exactly! Wow, he *is* smart!"

"He says you're the kind of girl who could join his gang. I can put your name forward, if you like."

"For sure!"

"Are you really sure? Because Jesse's gang is not like our little gang. You have to pay ten dollars to join. We have big plans."

Ten dollars...well, it was

a small price to pay to get
a little action in my life.

\* \* \*

The bus ride seemed endless.
I couldn't wait to
get home and check out how
much money was in my
piggybank.

Only one more stop. I signalled to my brothers in the
back of the bus and stood up.
"If you ask me over, I can

help you with your math," suggested Clementine.

Uh-oh! I knew where she was heading! She wanted me to confide in her.

"I'm getting off here too," said Patrick. "After we do our homework, we can play ball."

"Or maybe hopscotch!" sneered Nicholas.

"You'd better watch it. Pull too hard on the elastic," warned Patrick. "and it will snap back in your face."

Nicholas backed down. He had changed, but not enough to want to make Patrick mad.

As I got off the bus, I thought that our friendships were wearing out like an old elastic band, and our gang was about to snap apart.

Alexander and Julian pushed past me.

"Last one home gets no snack!"

What babies! I had more important things to do than gobble cookies.

I went in the house and walked through the kitchen without—

"Maddie! Aren't you going to say hello?"

"Gran! You're here. Uh, hello!"

"You seem a bit distracted."

"I have tons of homework," I said, to cut her questions off.

I knew what would have happened. I would have told her everything. I like Gran and she's been a big help to me. But I can't always hide behind her skirts. I have my own life to lead!

I went up to my room, tossed my bag on the floor, and started shaking out my piggybank. Six dollars and forty cents. That was all! Then I remembered why: I had raided the bank to buy the Zoozie record. Grrr!

* * *

Dipping my cookie in my milk, I gloomily considered the situation. You can't go far without any money. But even if I had enough money, it didn't mean Jesse would take me into his gang. I was stuck in the same old rut forever.

I took another cookie.

"That's enough, Maddie!" my mother interrupted my thoughts. "You'll spoil your appetite."

"I'm not even hungry now. I'm just eating cookies for something to do."

"I can tell you aren't feeling your best, sweetie-pie," said Gran.

When she called me that, it was too much. I felt like I was slipping back into babyhood. Soon I would be sucking on a bottle.

"Maddie! Alexander is calling you. The phone is for you."

I ran down to the basement.

"It's Nicholas," Alexander informed me.

I took the phone and made a sign to Alexander to leave. He didn't budge. Grrr!

"Hi, Nicholas...Really? Jesse said okay?...A meeting after school?...Yeah, I'll be there. With the money. Okay, bye!"

I was excited! The next day, I would be a member of Jesse's gang, as long as I played my cards right.

First, I warned Alexander. "Forget about Nicholas. That was Clementine on the phone, right?"

"Sure...if you give me your Zoozie CD."

Aaargh! I couldn't believe it! But I had to give in.

I went back up to the kitchen, repeating my first lie. "Clementine is going to help me with math after school tomorrow. Clementine is going..."

My mother agreed immediately. "When you're with Clementine, I know you'll be studying."

I was jubilant. That didn't last long.

"Gran's gone already!!!"

"Calm down! She's in the living room."

I went to the living room, repeating my next lie: "I *am* a bit down in the dumps. Some good music would cheer me up."

"I'd really like the Zoozie CD," I told Gran. "But I need ten dollars!"

"Hmmm," she said thoughtfully. "Well, good music is priceless. And I could listen to it, too."

What an inspiration, to choose a record I already had! It's amazing how easy it is to trick grown-ups.

All my problems were solved, so I let myself go a bit. I snuggled up next to Gran.

It felt awfully good with her arms around me. It's not that easy to cut the apron strings!

# 3
# A Different World

The meeting was to take place at Marco Siconelli's house. Marco was this shrimpy kid who always looked out of it.

"Jesse let *him* be in the gang!?" I asked Nicholas.

"He could see Marco's potential! And now Marco is an essential member. We meet at his house. His parents don't get home until six, and we can let ourselves go."

When we got there, I could see that Nicholas was right. A crowd of kids was dancing to the beat of wild music. All at once it stopped.

Jesse came over to us.

"To Maddie!" he cried. "Hip hip hop, YO!"

"HIP HIP HOP, YO!" yelled the others.

They were an amazing sight. I felt like a donkey in a herd of zebras. Some had tattoos, others had dyed hair, still others had rings through their noses, their lips, their eyebrows.

I felt totally insignificant.

"Don't worry," Jesse said, noticing my reaction. "Here, you can look however you like. Right, Nick?"

Everyone laughed. Nicholas turned cherry-red.

"My parents wouldn't like it," he stammered, "because

of the customers in the store."

"By the way," murmured Jesse. "Did you remember..."

"You know you can count on me!" cried Nicholas.

And he pulled a carton of cigarettes out of his bag! Jesse gave him the thumbs-up and turned to me.

His magnetic eyes seemed to be sending me a message. Oh! The ten dollars! What an idiot! How could I have forgotten! I handed the money over to Jesse, who waved it in the air.

"I was right about Maddie! She's a great addition to our gang! The first to invest in our new project!"

The others clamoured around him with questions.

He let the suspense build by stopping to light a cigarette.

"The giant concert of DEATHROCKERS!"

They went wild! Only Marco seemed disappointed.

"We should go see Zoozie instead," he muttered. "I like Zoozie better."

I was about to agree when Jesse answered.

"Zoozie is babyfood! Death-rockers rule!"

Everyone cheered. Fortunately I had kept my mouth shut, otherwise I would have looked pathetic.

"Of course, the tickets are more expensive," Jesse said. "We'll have to build up the kitty. I'll put in fifty."

Pandemonium broke out

again. He held up his hand.

"If you wish to contribute, I have everything you need right here," he said, unwrapping a small package.

"What is it?" I whispered to Nicholas.

"Tickets for a charity. We get a percentage of the sales."

"Are you going to take any?"

"No, I can make more money reselling candy and single cigarettes."

If I was going to maintain my reputation, I would have to outsell everyone else. I told Jesse I'd take two books of tickets. He gave me one thumb up.

After everyone got their tickets, he said he would sing

his new rap song. He was going to make a recording. That was amazing!

We would be the first to hear the new piece:

*Hip hop! Yo! Your life is your own. Make it what you will. Move, baby, move! Make your own revolution, make your own evolution. If you ain't you, yo, then you is who, yo? Your life is your own. Yeah baby it's your own.*

I was blown away.

Beep-beep! Beep-beep!

Grrr! Jesse's cell phone. He took the call but hung up almost immediately.

"Sorry, gang, I gotta go. We'll meet again in two weeks."

There was a wave of protests.

"We'll get the Deathrockers tickets then," he said to calm the outcry. "In the meantime, remember our code of silence. Otherwise the adults will start interfering in our projects. Hip hip hop, YO!"

"HIP HIP HOP, YO!" the gang yelled back. I yelled the loudest of all.

\* \* \*

Two weeks was plenty of time to sell my tickets. The urgent problem I had to deal with was how I looked.

"I'm going upstairs to study," I told my mom when I got home.

"More studying?" she was

astonished. "Clementine is having a very positive influence on you!"

I'd forgotten Little Miss Perfect. She seemed so far away. It was as if I had moved into a different world. I'd have to watch what I said.

I closed the bedroom door and set to work on my transformation.

I put on three unmatched t-shirts and an old pair of jeans of my mom's, which were way too big for me. I borrowed some ear-rings of hers too, and hung them in my nose. Using my dad's gel, I sculpted my hair into spikes.

Wow, wait till the next meeting! I'd knock 'em dead.

I put on the tape that

Nicholas had lent me. The
music of Deathrockers broke
out in an electric storm. I felt
myself pulled along willy-
nilly. My whole body started
twitching and shaking.

"Dabdoobadabong! Tapbedongbeedooyo."

Suddenly Julian burst in, followed by Alexander and my mother, then my dad with Angelbaby. Dad was covering her ears. I stopped the music to hear what my mother was shrieking.

"Are you out of your mind?"

I felt a bit dizzy, but I stammered, "What? I'm just developing my personality!"

"Go into the shower and wash off that personality," my father advised me. "When you come back, try looking like a human being."

"It's true, you do look like a monkey," said Alexander.

"Like a marmoset," Julian corrected him.

"Banana!" exclaimed Angelbaby.

Faced with my family's total lack of understanding, I retreated to the bathroom.

After my shower, I cheered up. I realized that my parents were stifling my development.

* * *

The next morning I told Nicholas about their reaction.

"You didn't tell them about our plans, did you?" he asked.

"Do you think I'm crazy? I obeyed the rule of silence! I should call Jesse and tell him. Do you have his number?"

"He never gives it out," said Nicholas. "Otherwise, people would be bugging him all the time. Well, bye. See you later. I have to go sell my cigarettes in the big kids' yard."

And he left me there just as the others came up.

"What are you two hatching?" asked Clementine, like a nosy mouse.

"You can't ever catch Nicholas anymore," remarked Patrick. "He's turned into a puff of wind."

"He's breaking free of you, and you don't like it, do you? He wants to see what else there is! And there's a lot more going on than stupid school and karate lessons, I can tell you!"

Take that, Little Miss Perfect.

"Such as?" she asked.

I was caught unprepared.

"I don't know! New challenges, or something!"

"Could you be more precise, please?" asked Clementine.

"We might be interested," added Patrick.

If I said nothing, I would look like an idiot. On the other hand, I couldn't tell them anything. But maybe I would! I didn't have to tell them *everything*.

"My current challenge is selling tickets for a charity!" I announced.

And believe it or not, I managed to sell each of them a ticket! Yo!

# 4
## The Bubble Bursts

Over the next two weeks,
I didn't sell a single other
ticket. I couldn't sell them
to my family without giving
away where they came from.
And at school Nicholas was
raking in all kinds of money
selling his candy at cut prices.

I asked him how the other
gang members managed to
sell their tickets.

"They do what Jesse said:
they go door-to-door in a big
apartment building."

Just thinking about it made
me shudder. Knocking on

strangers' doors, all alone! No way!

But I couldn't back down. The meeting was coming up the next day. I remembered what Jesse had said: "A girl who likes action. What a great addition to our gang. Make your own revolution. Move it, baby."

I told my mother I was going for a walk and I went out.

Once outside, I didn't walk—I ran! I ran into the first building I came to.

My heart thumping, I went up to a door and rang the bell. No answer. Whew!

I went down the dark, narrow corridor. At the next door my hand was shaking so much that it made the bell ring several times. Ah! Someone was coming. A man opened the door and yelled a string of insults at me, before slamming the door in my face.

Move it, baby! Move it, baby!

"What's going on here?"

An old lady opened her door and beckoned to me. I walked slowly over. I muttered that I was selling charity tickets.

"Come in," she said, pulling me inside.

Her crooked fingers gripped my arm. All of the fear I had been keeping inside burst out. I tore myself away. I ran out the door and down the hall, and shot out of the building

like a rocket.

I finally calmed down when I had landed back in my room. But I felt pathetic. I felt like Jesse's magnetic eyes were looking down at me in scorn.

There was only one solution left. I would have to use the six dollars in my piggybank and buy the tickets myself.

* * *

The whole gang was in the basement again, except Jesse. A sort of uneasiness hung over everyone. Nobody really knew anyone else. I didn't know anyone but Nicholas and Marco.

"Hip hip hop, yo!"

It was Jesse. The atmosphere perked up. Everyone crowded around him, jostling to hand in their money.

Apprehensively, I handed over my small stash. He made no comment. To think of all the heartache it gave me!

In the middle of the crush, a kid said, "Let's go buy the tickets now."

"Can't. I have to leave now," said Jesse. He seemed nervous. "Anyway, we don't have enough money. Go for it, guys! Just a bit more work, and we'll meet again at the end of the week! Hip hip—"

Beep-beep! The cell phone interrupted his rallying cry. Jesse gave us the thumbs-up and left.

The party went downhill from there. Some kids left. Others suggested putting on some music. But no one was very enthusiastic.

When I was walking home with Nicholas I told him what I thought.

"If we don't have enough money to go see Deathrockers, let's do something else!

Honestly, Jesse's a bust! He promises action, and then he just disappears! That meeting was a total drag!"

For a tiny instant, my thoughts flashed to my old friends. That was weird. I was so far beyond them.

"What's really a drag is that I don't have any candy," said Nicholas. "We'll talk to Jesse next time."

"I won't be coming next time. I can't keep on telling my mom I'm going to Clementine's."

"I told you this was no gang for babies," Nicholas reminded me.

He was lucky we had just gotten to my house, or else I would have told him...what?

Who knows?

I didn't know what to think anymore about all this. Jesse, his gang, his projects. I didn't even know who I was anymore. It was terrible. If I wasn't me, then who was I?

Deep in these reflections, I opened the door. Alexander was there, making wild faces and gestures. I was in no mood to figure out what they meant.

"There you are," said my mother in a strange voice.

She shooed Alexander away. Something was up, that was clear.

"Clementine called."

Yikes! I hit reality with a thud.

"Clementine thinks you've changed a lot, Maddie. And so do I. What's going on?"

I let her go on, imagining a hundred different scenarios, all light years from the truth. I kept waiting for the fatal question: "Where have you been?"

"It would do you good to talk about it," said my mother. "But I'm not going to twist your arm."

She had finished. I still

couldn't believe it as I went up to my room. I didn't understand.

Alexander was waiting upstairs and he filled me in.

"Clementine called and I answered the phone in the basement. I told her you were supposed to be studying at her house before Mom picked the phone up."

I would never have thought Alexander could do something so wonderful!

"But, you know, we're not always going to be able to cover for you. Stop, before it's too late, kid."

Any other time, I would have told him what he could do with his advice. But this time I agreed with him. I was struck by the enormity of what I'd done: the risks, the danger, the lies, the expense.

I would have even worse problems if I went any further. What a close call! And I escaped thanks only to Alexander...and Clementine. I'd have to thank her.

# 5
## Maddie Breaks the Code of Silence

Clementine was alone, leaning against the wall in the schoolyard, leafing through a book. I was sure she was going to deliver a lecture.

But no! She didn't snub me at all. She seemed to think it was normal to cover for me.

"I just told your mother that I was calling to let her know you were on your way."

She laughed at her cleverness, and I laughed along. It felt good. I was lucky to have such a great friend.

"No one else could have thought of that! You really are perfect!"

She turned pink with pleasure.

Then Patrick turned up. He was pink too—but not with pleasure.

"You cheated us," he roared. "You and those so-called friends of yours! You stole our money!"

He took out the ticket I had sold him and threw it in my face! He came up close to me, threatening, scary.

Clementine leapt into her karate position.

"Breathe through your nose, Patrick. It helps to bring oxygen to the brain. That's right. You'll need oxygen in

the brain so you can tell us
what you're talking about."

* * *

Patrick explained it all again
to the whole gang over at
Marco's house.
"Your charity tickets were
fake. I saw on TV that they

come from a well-organized network of petty thieves."

I remembered Jesse's cell phone.

"They lure kids into their scheme by promising them all kinds of things. Then they use them for swindling money."

When I found out the truth, I was furious too. That was it for the code of silence. Jesse would soon find out what I was made of! Yo!

I decided to expose him and to warn the others, with the help of my friends.

"Jesse won't show up," Clementine predicted. "The network is on the verge of being exposed."

"That must be why he was nervous the other day."

In Marco's basement, confusion reigned.

"He'll come," said Nicholas stubbornly. He was so disappointed, he just couldn't accept the truth. We decided to wait for Jesse.

Clementine readied herself by executing a few karate moves. The older kids were getting restless. Patrick went over to Nicholas, who was stuffing his face with candy. That was a good sign.

But as predicted, Jesse never showed up. No one knew how to track him down. We finally agreed that we would have to just try to forget about the whole thing. But we all swore we wouldn't be tricked again.

"Now I'll be all alone again," whimpered Marco as we left.

I promised that I would introduce him to a fantastic kid—my brother Alexander.

* * *

"Okay, okay," said Alexander after I had nagged him half to death. "I'll make friends with your little Marco."

I knew he would. He loves to feel important. Of course, I had to tell him the whole story, after swearing him to secrecy.

It was up to me to tell my parents. I figured the best bet was to go through Gran.

"You were very foolish,

Maddie. But that little crook inadvertently helped you. Now you know who your true friends are...and that you can't always trust the smooth talkers."

I snuggled against Gran. I was finally beginning to

relax when Julian stormed in.

"You are not nice! You never tell me any secrets! I want to help the little abandoned boy in the basement too!"

Grrr! Alexander had to show off to Julian! I figured by that time my parents knew everything there was to know. I would have to be prepared for strict supervision for quite a while!

But that wasn't so terrible. I was ready for a little bit of peace and quiet in my life anyway.

# Meet all the great kids in the *First Novels Series*!

## Meet Arthur—an only child with a great Dad

- *Arthur Throws a Tantrum*
- *Arthur's Dad*
- *Arthur's Problem Puppy*

## Meet Carrie—who is determined to try new things, no matter the results

- *Carrie's Crowd*
- *Go For It, Carrie*
- *Carrie's Camping Adventure*

## Meet Duff—always on the lookout for adventure

- *Duff's Monkey Business*
- *Duff the Giant Killer*

## Meet Fred—whose wild imagination and love of cats gets him into all kinds of trouble!

- *Fred on the Ice Floes*
- *Fred and the Food*
- *Fred and the Stinky Cheese*
- *Fred's Dream Cat*
- *Fred's Midnight Prowler*

## Meet Jan—resourceful Jan, whose persistence sometimes goes too far

- *Jan's Awesome Party*
- *Jan on the Trail*
- *Jan and Patch*
- *Jan's Big Bang*

## Meet Lilly—who likes to play with her friends and help out in her neighbourhood

- *Lilly's Good Deed*
- *Lilly Plays her Part*
- *Lilly to the Rescue*

## Meet the Loonies—pocket-size people who like to have fun

- *Loonie Summer*
- *The Loonies Arrive*

## Meet Maddie— irrepressible Maddie whose family is just too much sometimes

- *Maddie Needs her Own Life*
- *Maddie in Trouble*
- *Maddie Goes to Paris*
- *Maddie in Danger*
- *Maddie in Goal*
- *Maddie Tries to Be Good*
- *Maddie Wants Music*
- *Maddie Wants New Clothes*
- *That's Enough Maddie!*

## Meet Marilou—and her clan of clever friends

- *Marilou, Iguana Hunter*
- *Marilou on Stage*
- *Marilou's Long Nose*

## Meet Mikey—a small boy with a big problem

- *Mikey Mite's Best Present*
- *Good For You, Mikey Mite!*
- *Mikey Mite Goes to School*
- *Mikey Mite's Big Problem*

## Meet Mooch—and Carl, who is learning lessons about life thanks to his dog Mooch

- *A Gift from Mooch*
- *Missing Mooch*
- *Mooch Forever*
- *Hang On, Mooch!*
- *Mooch Gets Jealous*
- *Mooch and Me*
- *Life without Mooch*

**Meet Morgan—who always seems to be in the right place at the wrong time**

- *Great Play, Morgan*
- *Morgan's Secret*
- *Morgan and the Money*
- *Morgan Makes Magic*
- *Great Play, Morgan*

**Meet Robyn—an only child who is looking for ways to have more fun**

- *Robyn's Best Idea*
- *Robyn Looks for Bears*
- *Robyn's Want Ad*
- *Shoot for the Moon, Robyn*

**Meet the Swank Twins—who do everything together**

- *The Swank Prank*
- *Swank Talk*

**Meet other First Novel friends**

- *Leo and Julio*
- *Max the Superhero*
- *Will and His World*
- *Video Rivals*

**Formac Publishing Company Limited**
*5502 Atlantic Street,*
*Halifax, Nova Scotia*
*B3H 1G4*
*www.formac.ca*
*Orders: 1-800-565-1975*
*Fax: (902) 425-0166*